THE GIFT OF THE SACRED DOG

THE GIFT OF THE SACRED DOG

Story and Illustrations by PAUL GOBLE

Aladdin Books
Macmillan Publishing Company
New York

About the title:

Horses were brought to North America by the Spanish. To the tribes of nomadic buffalo hunters who lived on the Great Plains, horses were truly miraculous. This wonderful animal could not only carry and drag far heavier burdens than their dogs, but could also carry a rider and run faster than anyone ever imagined. The tribes call him by various names: Big Dog, Elk Dog, Mysterious Dog, Holy or Sacred Dog. They tell factual accounts of the first horses they saw, but the story is told as well in ways which remind that Sacred Dogs were indeed given by the Great Spirit.

I would like to thank Mike Cowdrey for helping me with some thoughts and details for the illustrations. — P.G.

Copyright © 1980 by Paul Goble

Aladdin Books
Macmillan Publishing Company
866 Third Avenue, New York, NY 10022
Collier Macmillan Canada, Inc.

First Aladdin Books edition 1987

Printed in the United States of America

A hardcover edition of The Gift of the Sacred Dog *is available from Bradbury Press, an affiliate of Macmillan, Inc.*

10   9   8   7   6   5   4

Library of Congress Cataloging-in-Publication Data
Goble, Paul.
   The gift of the sacred dog / by Paul Goble.—1st Aladdin Books ed.
      p.   cm.
   Summary: In response to an Indian boy's prayer for help for his hungry people, the Great Spirit sends the gift of the Sacred Dogs, horses, which enable the tribe to hunt for buffalo.
   ISBN 0-02-043280-1 : $4.95
   1. Indians of North America—Great Plains—Legends. [1. Indians of North America—Great Plains—Legends. 2. Horses—Folklore.] I. Title.
[E78.G73G6 1987]
398.2′08997078—dc19
[E]

For Mother and Bobbie

The people were hungry. They had walked many days looking for the buffalo herds. Each day they hoped to see the buffalo over the next ridge, but they were not to be found in that part of the country. Even the buzzards and crows circled looking for something to eat, and the wolves called out with hunger at night. The people wandered on until they were too tired and hungry to go any farther, and the dogs could no longer be urged to drag their heavy loads.

The wise men said that they must dance to bring back their relatives, the buffalo. Every man who had dreamed of the buffalo joined in the dance. The buffalo would surely know the people needed them. Young men went out searching in all directions but they did not see any buffalo herds.

There was a boy in the camp who was sad to hear his little brothers and sisters crying with hunger. He saw his mother and father eat nothing so that the children could have what little food there was.

He told his parents: "I am sad to see everyone suffering. The dogs are hungry too. I am going up into the hills to ask the Great Spirit to help us. Do not worry about me; I shall return in the morning."

He left the circle of tipis and walked toward the hills. He climbed higher and higher. The air was cool and smelled fresh with pine trees.

He reached the top of the highest hill as the sun was setting. He raised his arms and spoke: "Great Spirit, my people need your help. We follow the buffalo herds because you gave them to us. But we cannot find them and we can walk no farther. We are hungry. My little brothers and sisters are crying. Great Spirit, we need your help."

As he stood there on the hilltop, great clouds closed across the sky. Wind and hail came with sudden force, and behind them Thunderbirds swooped among the clouds. Lightning darted from their flashing eyes and thunder rumbled when they flapped their enormous wings. He felt afraid and wondered if the Great Spirit had answered him.

The clouds parted. Someone came riding toward the boy on the back of a beautiful animal. There was thunder in its nostrils and lightning in its legs; its eyes shone like stars and hair on its neck and tail trailed like clouds.

The boy had never seen any animal so magnificent.

The rider spoke: "I know your people are in need. They will receive this: he is called Sacred Dog because he can do many things your dogs can do, and also more. He will carry you far and will run faster than the buffalo. He comes from the sky. He is as the wind: gentle but sometimes frightening. Look after him always."

The clouds closed and the rider was not there. Suddenly the sky was filled with Sacred Dogs of all colors and the boy could never count their number. Their galloping was like the wind and the drumming of their hoof beats shook the hilltop on which he stood. They circled round and round and he did not know if he was standing or falling.

He did not remember going to sleep, but he awoke as the sun was rising. He knew it was something wonderful he had seen in the sky. He started down the hill back home again to ask the wise men what it meant. They would be able to tell him. The morning and everything around him was beautiful and good.

When the boy had reached the level plain he heard a sound like far-away thunder coming from the hill behind. Looking back he saw Sacred Dogs pouring out of a cave and coming down a ravine toward him. They were of all colors, just as he had seen in the sky, galloping down the slopes, neighing and kicking up their back legs with excitement.

The leading ones stopped when they were a short distance away. They stamped their feet and snorted, but their eyes were gentle too, like those of the deer. The boy knew they were what he had been promised on the hilltop. He turned and continued walking toward the camp and all the Sacred Dogs followed him.

The people were excited and came out from the camp circle when they saw the boy returning with so many strange and beautiful animals. He told them; "These are Sacred Dogs. They are a gift from the Great Spirit. They will help us to follow the buffalo and they will carry the hunters into the running herds. Now there will always be enough to eat. We must look after them well and they will be happy to live with us."

Life was good after that. The people lived as relatives with the Sacred Dogs, together with the buffalo and all other living things, as the Great Spirit wished them to live.

When the people passed the place where they had hunted the buffalo, they would gather up the bleached skulls in a circle and face them toward the sun. "Let us thank the spirits of the buffalo who died so that we could eat."

A Sioux song for the return of the buffalo:
The whole world is coming,
A Nation is coming, a Nation is coming,
The Eagle has brought the message to the tribe,
The Father says so, the Father says so.
Over the whole earth they are coming,
The Buffalo are coming, the Buffalo are coming,
The Crow has brought the message to the tribe,
The Father says so, the Father says so.

Sioux songs of horses:
Friend
my horse
flies like a bird
as it runs.

The four winds are blowing;
some horses
are coming.

Daybreak
appears
when
a horse
neighs.